Cathy Bellows

TOAD SCHOOL

Macmillan Publishing Company
New York

Collier Macmillan Publishers
London

To my sisters,
Cynthia and Suzanne

Macmillan Publishing Company
866 Third Avenue, New York, NY 10022
Collier Macmillan Canada, Inc.
Printed and bound in Hong Kong
First American Edition

10 9 8 7 6 5 4 3 2 1

The text of this book is set in 16 point Horley Old Style.
The illustrations are rendered in watercolor.

Library of Congress Cataloging-in-Publication Data
Bellows, Cathy.
Toad school/Cathy Bellows. — 1st American ed.
p.   cm.
Summary: A young toad who sees no point in what she learns at school
soon discovers that the lessons are invaluable for getting through life.
ISBN 0-02-708835-9
[1. Toads — Fiction. 2. Life skills — Fiction.]   I. Title.
PZ7.B415 1990   [E] — dc20   89-12562 CIP AC

Once there was a toad who didn't want to go to school. Her parents begged and pleaded and gave her beautiful new school clothes, but still she didn't want to go.

"Why can't I stay here at the bottom of the pond?" asked Polly. "Why can't I just swim around the way I always do?"

"And grow up without a proper education?" Mr. and Mrs. Wog gasped. Why, they'd never heard of such an awful thing! So they did what parents sometimes do when their children don't want to go to school: They picked her up and carried her off.

Across the pond they swam till they came to a large flat lily pad covered with tiny toads. There, in the center, sat the wise old toad teacher, Miss Lilywart.

"I see we have a new student," said Miss Lilywart as Polly's parents plunked her down and waved good-bye. "What is your name, my dear?"

"Polly Wog," said Polly, "and if you don't mind, I'll just go back down to the bottom of the pond."

Miss Lilywart, however, would have none of that. "Surely you don't want to miss croaking class, do you?" she said. Then she clapped her hands, and all the little toads looked up. "All right, children, let's croak our heads off!"

Well, Polly had never heard such an awful noise. Those little toads croaked and creaked and made such a terrible racket that Polly had to cover her ears. What kind of school is this? she wondered.

Just when she thought she could stand it no more, Miss Lilywart clapped her hands and everyone was quiet. "Excellent croaking!" said Miss Lilywart. "Now, class, let's practice our puffing."

So the little toads stood in a circle and began
to puff. They huffed and they puffed till they
almost blew themselves up. All except Polly,
that is.

What a silly school! she thought. What's the
point of all this puffing? And instead of puffing,
she opened her lunch box and munched on a
mosquito sandwich.

Worse, however, was yet to come. For then they had the most difficult lesson of all. Two by two, the little toads swam to the edge of the pond, where Miss Lilywart sat, looking very serious. "Children," she began, "what do you do if you're chased by monsters?"

The little toads looked at one another and shook their heads. They didn't know what to do.

"Well, then," said Miss Lilywart, "I shall show you." She knelt down low, scrunching on her hands and knees. Then *boing!* Up into the air she flew!

Boing! Boing! Boing! Through the reeds she leaped, faster and faster, higher and higher, forward and backward, and even around in circles. *Boing! Boing!* It was a marvelous sight! The little toads were very impressed.

"Come, children," cried Miss Lilywart. "Now you try!"

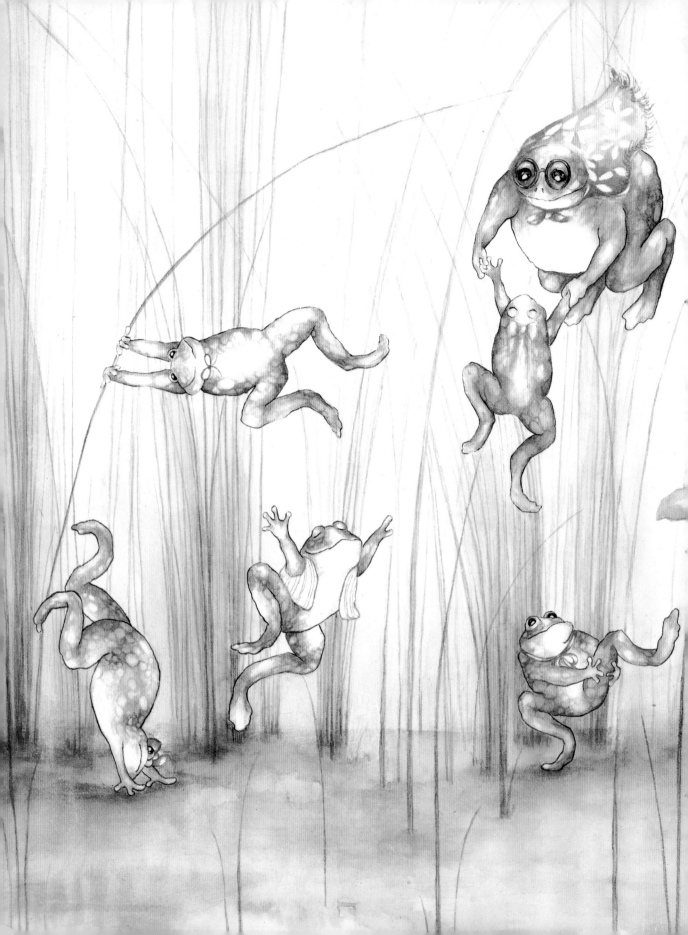

The toads tried to follow Miss Lilywart as she *boinged* along. They plopped and fell and rolled, and sometimes they *boinged*. They weren't good at first, but they practiced and practiced and tried to get better. All except Polly, that is. She decided right away that all that *boinging* was too hard for her. So she lay under a marshmallow and took a little nap.

"Class dismissed!" said Miss Lilywart, and Polly awoke with a start.

Thank goodness! she thought. Now I can finally go back to the bottom of the pond. But just as she was about to dive into the water, Miss Lilywart said, "Miss Polly Wog! Will you come to my lily pad, please?"

Pooey! thought Polly. I want to go home!

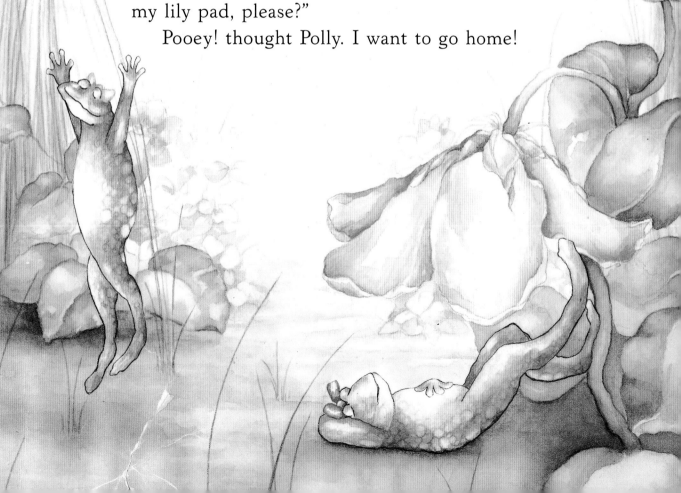

"My dear," began Miss Lilywart, "I know this
is only your first day, but you really must try a
little harder. Now, I want you to stay after school
and practice what we learned today. If you need
any help, I'll be right here on my pad, doing my
lesson plans."

"Yes, Miss Lilywart," said Polly Wog. Then
she sat on the edge of the lily pad and began to
sulk. I'm not going to practice all that stuff! she
decided. It's too hard for me! I can't do all those
silly toady things! I'm going home! So she quietly
slipped off the pad and slid into the water.

Across the bottom of the pond she tiptoed, hoping Miss Lilywart wouldn't notice she was gone. But when she'd gotten halfway across, she suddenly felt something tickling her back. Turning around, she saw a big ugly catfish with long creeping whiskers.

"Pardon me," said the catfish with a gurgle, "but may I have a bite of your tiny toady toes?"

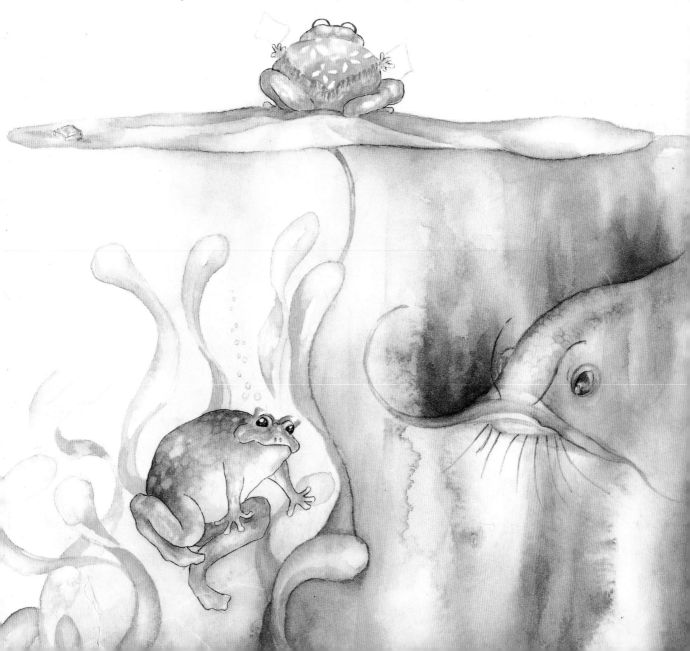

"Eeek!" cried Polly, and up to the surface she swam.

"Miss Lilywart!" she shouted as she climbed onto a reed. "Miss Lilywart! Come and get me!" Then she croaked as loudly as she could.

Miss Lilywart thought she heard a little toad croaking, but when she looked around, she couldn't see Polly anywhere. "That's very good croaking, my dear," yelled Miss Lilywart. "But you'll have to croak more loudly if you want me to hear what you're saying."

This is ridiculous! thought Polly. What do I have to do, croak my head off?

As Polly clung to the reed, trying to croak more loudly, two herons began circling overhead.

"You must try, my dear," squawked the mother heron to her son. "How will you ever learn if you don't try?"

"But, Mama," cried the heron, "it's so big!"

"Nonsense!" said his mother.

Polly looked up to see the young heron swoop down and snap at her with his beak.

"Help!" cried Polly. She tried to hide under a leaf, but it was too late. The heron picked her up in his beak, and into the air he flew.

"Let go of me!" she cried. "Please, let go!"

The young heron was quite proud of himself, so he fluttered around the pond showing everyone his toad.

"Miss Lilywart!" cried Polly as she dangled in the air. "Miss Lilywart, save me!"

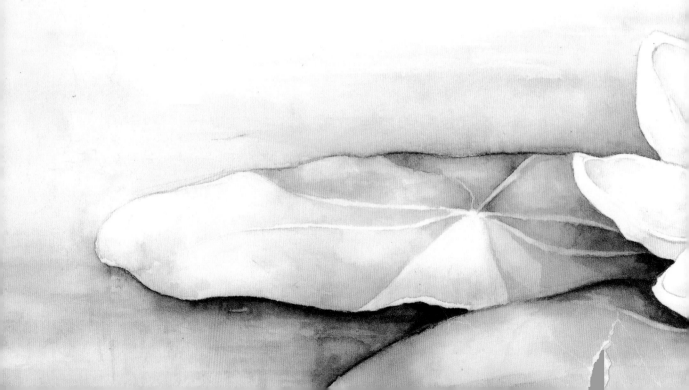

Miss Lilywart looked up just as Polly went flying by. "Don't panic, my dear," called Miss Lilywart. "Stay calm and practice your puffing!"

Practice my puffing? thought Polly. That's the silliest thing I've ever heard. She was so angry that she began to huff and huff until, finally, she puffed. It wasn't much of a puff, but it was enough.

"Ouch!" cried the heron. "Stop that puffing! You're hurting my beak!" And, dropping the little toad, he quickly flew back to his mama.

"Ouch!" cried Polly as she landed—*klunk!*—in a bright bed of snapdragons. Well, who would have thought puffing could be so useful? Certainly not Polly!

Nevertheless, she'd had quite enough of school, and she decided right then and there never to go back. "I shall find myself a new pond," she said, "far away from Mama and Papa and Miss Lilywart." So, instead of heading home, she turned toward the snapdragons and soon found herself in the middle of a thick garden.

What a journey! She trudged through bellflowers and lilies and irises and daisies, until she came upon a great green lawn. There, in the middle of the grass, sat three little dollies having a tea party.

Water! thought Polly, and she headed straight for the cups.

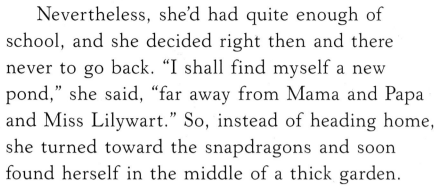

Sure enough, the dollies' cups were full of water, and Polly plopped herself down in one for a nice cool soak. "At last," she said, "I've found my new home! I shall stay here forever and ever and never go back to that horrid toad school." Then she curled up in the cup, as cozy as could be, and slowly drifted off to sleep.

Meanwhile, in the house nearby, the children had just finished their lunch and were coming back outside to play. Through the garden they skipped, and, sitting down near the little tea set, they prepared to drink their pretend tea.

"Won't you have a cup of tea, my dear?" said one of the little girls.

"Thank you very much, my dear," said her friend. Then she picked up a teacup. "Eeek!" she cried. "A toad!"

"Eeek!" cried Polly. "Monsters!"

Quickly the children ran off into the house, and just as quickly Polly hid under her teacup.

Monsters! she thought. I've never seen such ugly giants in my whole life. Teeth in their mouths and fur on their heads, and, oh, those noses! Why, the very thought of them sent shivers down her warts.

I must escape before they come back, Polly thought. There's no telling what they might do to me. She tried to remember what Miss Lilywart had taught her. If you're ever chased by monsters, you have to—oh, yes!—*boing*!

Across the lawn she leaped, heading for the
tall grass beyond. *Hoppity-clunk! Hoppity-clunk!*
Hoppity-plunk! Try as she might, she kept falling
over. She wasn't halfway across the lawn, when,
suddenly, the girls came out again. This time,
however, they were carrying a big glass jar.

"Let's see if we can catch it!" cried one of the girls. "But don't touch it, or you'll get warts!"

They're trying to steal my warts! thought Polly. This was serious! Jumping onto her hind legs, she decided she was going to have to make a *boing* for it.

Hoppity-clunk! Hoppity-clunk! The children were getting closer.

Hoppity-clunk! Hoppity-clunk! Hoppity-boing!

Yes! *Boing!* Polly *boinged* into the tall grass in the nick of time.

"Stop that hopping, you stupid toad!" cried the children as they chased her though the grass.

But little Polly wouldn't stop. *Boing! Boing! Boing!* She flew through the air as fast as could be. "You can't catch me!" she shouted. "I've been to toad school!"

Across the marsh she sailed. *Boing! Boing! Boing!* In no time at all, she was back in the pond.

Miss Lilywart looked up to see Polly—*boing!*—land right in the middle of her lily pad. Into the water they plunged, down to the bottom of the pond. Then up to the surface they surged.

"Excellent!" said Miss Lilywart as they climbed onto another pad. "Wonderful leaping, my dear, simply wonderful! You see what a little practice can do? Why, if you keep practicing like this, I won't be a bit surprised if you graduate at the top of your class!"

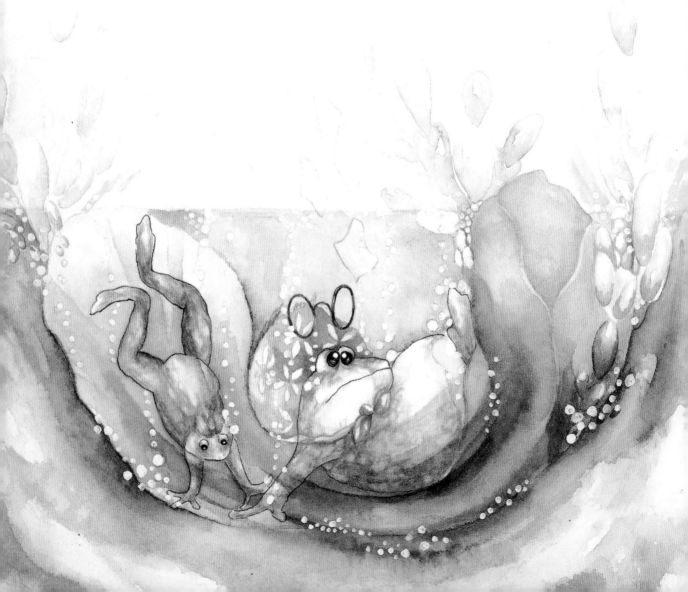

"Really!" Polly gasped.

"Yes, indeed," said Miss Lilywart. "Now you must go home and rest, my dear, for tomorrow is going to be a very busy day. I've decided to teach fly catching tomorrow."

"Fly catching!" cried Polly. "Oh, Miss Lilywart, I've always wanted to learn how to catch flies. But, tell me, is it hard? Is it too hard for me?"

"Certainly not!" said Miss Lilywart. "It just takes practice, that's all."

"Practice?" said Polly. "I can do that! I can try!"

And all the way home she leaped.
Boing! Boing! Boing!